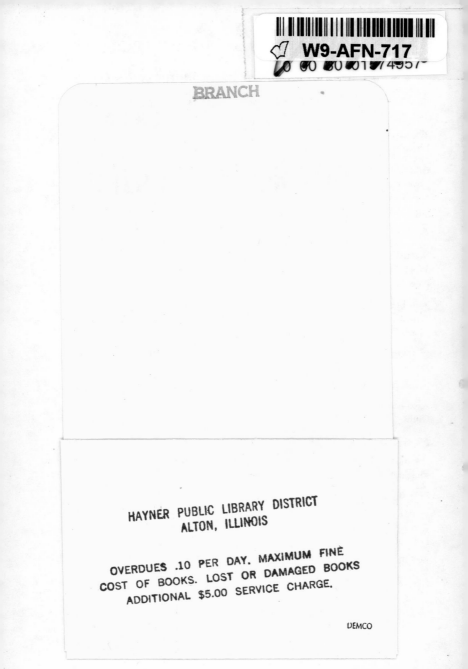

To Prince and his best friend. BBC

For both Bills and their two wondrous gifts. DMD

Text copyright © 1994 by Christina Lowenstein
Illustrations copyright © 1994 by Daniel Mark Duffy

Book design by Debora Smith

Scientific American Books for Young Readers is an imprint of
W. H. Freeman and Company, 41 Madison Avenue
New York, New York 10010

This book was reviewed for scientific accuracy by Don Lessem, founder of The Dinosaur Society.

Library of Congress Cataloging-in-Publication Data

Calhoun, B. B., 1961—

Bite Makes Right / B. B. Calhoun [i.e. Christina Lowenstein]: illustrations by Daniel Mark Duffy.

p. cm. –(Dinosaur detective : #3)

Summary: Fenton Rumplemayer, his friends, and a stray dog help Dr. Rumplemayer identify some mysterious dinosaur bones from Sleeping Bear Mountain.

ISBN 0-7167-6542-X —ISBN 0-7167-6550-0 (pbk.)

[1. Dinosaurs—Fiction. 2. Dogs—Fiction. 3. Paleontology—Fiction. 4. Fathers and sons—Fiction. 5. Mystery and detective stories.] I. Duffy, Daniel M., ill. II. Title. III. Series: Lowenstein, Christina. Dinosaur detective: #3

PZ7.C12744Bi 1994

[Fic]—dc20   94-16086
                                                                                                     CIP
                                                                                                      AC

Printed in the United States of America.

10 9 8 7 6 5 4 3 2 1

3 DINOSAUR DETECTIVE
Bite Makes Right

B. B. Calhoun

illustrated by Daniel Mark Duffy

Scientific

BOOKS FOR YOUNG READERS

American

W. H. FREEMAN AND COMPANY ◆ NEW YORK

1

"Ugh," said Fenton Rumplemayer as the egg he was cracking ran over his hands and into the bowl on the counter. "I think I got some shell in the batter."

"That ought to make the cookies nice and crunchy," said Maggie Carr, laughing. She popped another handful of chocolate chips into her mouth. "Okay, what do we do next, Willy?"

Willy Whitefox lifted the bag of chocolate chips off the counter and looked at the recipe on the back. "'Add the chips and stir well,'" he read. "That is, the chips that are *left*."

He looked at Maggie.

"Hey," said Maggie, "I can't help it if cooking makes me hungry."

Fenton took the bag of chocolate chips, poured it into the bowl of batter on the counter, and began to stir. He was pretty hungry too. When Willy had suggested that the three of them come over after school and make cookies, Fenton had agreed right away. Willy's household always seemed so warm and busy. Mrs. Whitefox was a kindergarten teacher, so she got

5

home from work early, and Willy's little sister, Jane, was usually playing somewhere nearby. Fenton knew his own house next door would be empty until later in the evening, when his father got home from work.

Mr. Rumplemayer was a paleontologist, a scientist who studies fossils, and he often worked long hours out at Sleeping Bear Mountain, where he was in charge of a dinosaur dig site. Fenton's mother, who was also a paleontologist, was in India, where she had a special grant to study dinosaur bones for a year. Fenton didn't really mind the fact that there usually wasn't anyone at home when he got back from school—he generally just made himself a snack and sat down in front of the computer or with one of his dinosaur books—but it definitely was a nice change to go to Willy's and make cookies.

Just then Willy's little sister, Jane, came into the kitchen, cuddling her orange kitten in her arms.

"Hey, what are you guys doing?" she asked.

Willy sighed. "What does it look like we're doing, Jane? We're baking."

"Yeah, and if you ask me, we're doing way too much baking and not enough eating," said Maggie. "When are these cookies going to be ready, anyway?"

"Cookies, yum!" said Jane, shifting her kitten to the other arm. "Can I help make them?"

"Sorry, Jane," said Willy. "You're too late. We're practically finished."

Jane pouted. "That's not fair." She looked at Fenton. "Fenkon, you'll let me help, won't you?"

Fenton thought a moment. He liked Jane, even though she always got his name wrong.

"Sure," he said. "Why don't you stir the batter for a minute?"

Willy scowled. "Fenton, the batter's already stirred."

Fenton shrugged. "It's probably okay if she stirs it a little more."

"Boy," sighed Maggie. "I'm starting to think these cookies are *never* going to be finished."

"Thanks, Fenkon," said Jane, taking the spoon from him. "Here, hold Simonetta for me."

Fenton took the squirming orange kitten from Jane's arms. It swiped at him with its paws, and he could feel its claws through his T-shirt.

"Ouch!" he said, grimacing and holding the kitten away from his body.

"Be careful, Fenkon!" cried Jane. "Don't drop her!"

"Okay, okay, don't worry," said Fenton, pulling the kitten in closer. He knew how much Simonetta meant to Jane.

And the kitten was very cute, Fenton had to admit. Now that it had settled into his arms and begun to purr, he thought he understood why Jane felt the way she did about it.

Five minutes later, Jane had finished stirring the batter, and the cookies were in the oven.

"Hey, Fenton," said Willy, sitting down at the kitchen table and picking up a Frisbee that was lying there. "What's going on out at the dig site these days?" He tossed the Frisbee into the air and caught it.

"My father and Charlie and Professor Martin have been doing some digging in a new area," said Fenton, "but so far they haven't found any fossils."

"Well, just as long as they haven't *lost* any, either," joked Maggie.

Fenton laughed. He knew that Maggie was referring to the most recent dinosaur find at Sleeping Bear Mountain. An important fossil had been lost, and it had been up to Fenton, Maggie, and Willy to solve the mystery of what had happened to it.

A few minutes later Mrs. Whitefox walked into the kitchen.

"Mmm," she said, sniffing. "Those cookies smell just about done to me." She opened the oven. "Sure, they're ready."

"Thank goodness," said Maggie, hopping up from her seat. "I'm starved."

Mrs. Whitefox watched as Willy pulled the trays of cookies out of the oven.

"It looks like you kids did a great job with these," she said.

"I helped too," said Jane, her eyes shining.

"Hey, you guys," said Willy, lifting the hot cookies from a baking sheet with a spatula, "I have an idea. Let's take our cookies out to the shack, okay?"

8

"Okay," said Fenton.

"Cool," said Maggie.

The shack was a little wooden building halfway between Fenton's and Willy's houses, where Willy kept his comic-book collection. Willy had more comic books than anyone Fenton had ever met.

"I want to come too," said Jane.

"No way," said Willy.

"That's not fair!" said Jane, pouting.

"Jane, honey, why don't you stay here with me," said Mrs. Whitefox.

Jane's lower lip began to tremble. "But I don't want to . . ." she whined.

"You know, it looks to me like Simonetta might be in the mood for a saucer of milk," said Mrs. Whitefox. "What do you think?"

Jane looked at the kitten, who was still asleep in Fenton's arms.

"I guess so," she said.

"Why don't we find out," said Mrs. Whitefox, opening the refrigerator.

"Okay," said Jane, taking the kitten from Fenton and walking over to her mother.

Willy picked up his Frisbee and spread out a paper napkin inside it. He put a bunch of the warm cookies on top.

"Come on, guys, let's go," he said, heading toward the door with the Frisbee full of cookies.

Fenton looked at Jane, wondering if she would ask to go with them again, but she was so busy holding a saucer of milk up to Simonetta's face that she didn't even seem to notice that they were leaving.

A few minutes later, Fenton, Maggie, and Willy were sitting in the shack, eating cookies from the Frisbee and looking through the stacks of comic books.

"Hey, you guys, check out this new issue of *Monster Mania* I just got," said Willy, holding up a comic book.

The cover picture showed two monsters fighting each other. The larger of the monsters had a double row of sharp spikes running down its back, and it was sinking its huge, bloody fangs into the neck of the smaller monster. The smaller one was fighting back by swinging its long tail, which had a big club at the end of it.

"Wow," said Fenton, chewing a cookie. "Whoever drew that picture was definitely into dinosaurs."

"What are you talking about?" asked Willy.

"Just look," said Fenton. "Those spikes on the big monster are straight off a kentrosaurus."

"Hey, yeah," said Maggie. "You're right, Fen."

"Really?" asked Willy.

"Sure," said Fenton. "Kentrosaurus was one of the stegosaurid dinosaurs, like stegosaurus. Except that instead of having plates running down its back, it had spikes."

"Cool," said Willy, taking a bite of a cookie.

"Of course, all the stegosaurids were vegetarians, though," Maggie pointed out. "So you probably wouldn't see one attacking like that."

"True," agreed Fenton. "But I guess that's because these are supposed to be monsters, not dinosaurs. I definitely think that whoever made this comic book knew something about dinosaurs, though. Look at that other monster's tail; it looks like it could be from one of the ankylosaurids."

"I see what you mean," said Maggie.

"The ankylosaurids," repeated Willy. "Which ones were those again?"

"They were four-footed plant-eaters that lived during the Cretaceous Period," explained Fenton. "And they all had these cool heavy bony clubs on the ends of their tails. They may have used them for defense."

"Wow," said Willy, looking down at the cover appreciatively.

"Hey, Willy," said Maggie, sorting through a pile of comic books, "what happened to that one you had about the horse— *The Wild Stallion*?"

"It's over here," said Fenton, reaching for a comic book

with a picture of a fierce-looking black horse rearing up on its hind legs. He tossed it to her.

"Maggie, haven't you read that one about a million times already?" asked Willy.

Maggie shrugged. "It's my favorite."

Fenton smiled. Maggie loved horses. Her family raised them on their ranch, and she even had her own horse, named Pepper.

Fenton looked through the pile of comic books in front of him and picked one up. It was called *Powerboy and Lightning*, and the cover picture showed a boy in a black cape with a large white dog by his side. He grabbed another cookie from the Frisbee and opened up the comic book.

Powerboy turned out to be an ordinary boy by day who turned into a superhero who fought the forces of evil at night. His trusty dog, Lightning, had secret superpowers too, and was always at his side. In this episode, Powerboy and Lightning had to stop some bank robbers. Lightning did some pretty amazing things, for a dog—like chewing through the ropes that the robbers had used to tie up Powerboy, and then attacking one of the villains and knocking his gun out of his hand.

Fenton finished the comic book, closed it, and popped the last piece of his cookie into his mouth.

"That was a cool story," he said. "Do you have any more of those, Willy?"

"Which?" asked Willy.

"*Powerboy and Lightning,*" said Fenton.

"Oh, you mean the one with the dog?" said Willy. He looked through a pile of comic books and pulled one out. "Sure, here," he said, holding it out to Fenton.

"Actually," said Fenton, looking at his watch, "maybe I'd better read it next time. I should probably go. My dad'll be home from work any minute."

"Yeah, I have to get home, too," said Maggie, standing up.

"You can take this *Powerboy* comic with you if you want, Fenton," said Willy.

"Really?" said Fenton.

"Sure," said Willy. "Just give it back to me when you're done." He looked at Maggie. "Sorry I don't have any more *Wild Stallion*s. You can borrow that one if you want, though."

"Nah, thanks anyway," said Maggie. "I practically know it by heart now."

"I think I will take this," said Fenton, picking up the *Powerboy* comic. "Thanks, Willy."

"No problem," said Willy as the three of them headed outside. "See you guys soon."

"Okay," said Fenton.

"Later," said Maggie, climbing onto her bike and heading down the driveway.

2

Fenton waved to Willy, tucked the comic book under his arm, and started down the path between the pine trees. He could see his own white house in the distance, and the mountains beyond it. It was kind of nice, thought Fenton, the way you could see the mountains from just about anywhere in Morgan. When he and his father had first moved to Wyoming from New York City this past summer, it had seemed really strange to be surrounded by mountains and trees and grass instead of tall buildings. But the more time Fenton spent in Morgan, the more used to it he became.

Just then Fenton thought he heard a rustle from the trees behind him. He stopped and turned around to look, but nothing was there. Probably it was just a squirrel scurrying by, he thought, starting to walk again.

Then he heard the noise again. This was definitely no squirrel; it sounded like something much bigger. He stopped again and turned around. Nothing.

"Who's there?" he called. "Willy? Is that you?"

There was no answer.

Fenton was starting to think about wild animals when out of the trees trotted a dog. It was light brown with thick fur and floppy ears. It ran right up to Fenton and sniffed his foot, its tail wagging.

"Hey there," said Fenton, crouching down and holding his hand out to the dog, "where did you come from?"

The dog sniffed Fenton's hand once and began to lick it.

"Hi, fella," said Fenton, scratching the dog behind the ears. "Are you lost or something? Where's your owner?"

He looked around, but no one was there. There was nothing in sight but trees and the mountains in the distance.

The dog licked Fenton's hand again and trotted back off into the trees. Oh well, thought Fenton, starting to walk again. I guess he's headed home. But a few moments later the dog reappeared at his side, holding a stick in its mouth. Fenton stopped, and the dog dropped the stick at his feet.

"You want to play, huh?" said Fenton, picking up the stick.

The dog barked once and jumped up, putting its front paws on Fenton's legs. It was almost as if he could understand what Fenton was saying.

"Okay, fella," said Fenton, "go get it." He tossed the stick a few yards away.

The dog ran off, grabbed the stick in its mouth, and brought it back to Fenton, dropping it at his feet.

"Good boy," said Fenton, reaching down to pick up the stick and patting the dog on the head. The dog looked up at him expectantly, its tail wagging.

"Okay," said Fenton, lifting the stick high in the air, "let's see you get this one." He threw the stick as hard as he could, and it sailed through the air into the trees. The dog took off.

Fenton waited, wondering what had happened to the dog. Gee, he thought, maybe I shouldn't have thrown the stick so far. It would probably be impossible to find it in the trees.

But then the dog came bounding out from between the trees, waving the stick in its mouth. It ran up to Fenton, its tail wagging, and dropped the stick at his feet.

"Good boy," said Fenton, smiling. This was some dog; it would probably make a great pet. For a moment Fenton imagined taking the dog home with him and adopting it. It could sleep on the floor near his bed, and they could play fetch together in the backyard, and Fenton could teach it tricks.

But no, there was no way his father would ever let him keep it; Fenton knew that. He had asked for a dog for years, but his parents had always refused. A dog was too much trouble, they said, too much responsibility. Finally Fenton had just given up.

Fenton sighed. Oh well, he thought, chances are it already had a home somewhere nearby anyway.

"So long, fella," he said, patting the dog once more.

The dog looked down at the stick on the ground and whined a little.

"Sorry, I can't play with you anymore," said Fenton.

The dog whined some more; it looked down at the stick again and back up at Fenton.

"Go home," Fenton repeated, waving his arm at the dog. "Go on!" He turned and began walking away from the dog.

He heard another low whimper behind him. He turned to look, and the dog pricked up its ears and wagged its tail a little.

Fenton walked back to it and scratched it behind the ears. The dog licked his hand.

"Sorry, fella, I have to go home now," Fenton said firmly.

Trying to ignore the sad feeling that was building up inside him, Fenton turned and walked quickly away down the path without looking back.

3

"Well, Fenton," said Mr. Rumplemayer as the two of them sat at the kitchen table eating dinner later that night, "it looks like we may have found something pretty interesting out at the dig site."

"Oh yeah?" said Fenton, buttering his corn. "What is it, Dad?"

"Well, from what we can see, there appear to be several pieces of some sort of dinosaur spine," said Fenton's father.

"Wow," said Fenton, taking a bite of his hamburger. "What kind of dinosaur are the pieces from?"

"We're not sure yet," said his father. "I guess we'll have to wait and see if we uncover some more of the animal before we can tell."

Fenton thought a moment. "Do you know how old the fossils are?" he asked. He knew that determining when a dinosaur had lived was often an important first step in figuring out what kind it had been.

"Not yet," said his father, shaking his head. "But Professor Martin is working on analyzing a piece of the surrounding rock, so we should have an idea by tomorrow."

"Cool," said Fenton. "I guess I'll ride out to the dig site tomorrow and take a look. How big are the spine bones you found, Dad? Do they give you any idea of how big the dinosaur may have been?"

"Actually, they're fairly small," said Mr. Rumplemayer. "My guess is that the dinosaur they're from probably wouldn't have stood any taller than my waist."

"Hmmm," said Fenton, chewing on his corn.

He thought about some of the smaller dinosaurs he knew of and tried to remember which ones had lived in the Wyoming area. There was ornitholestes, a two-legged meat-eater from the Late Jurassic Period, about 160 to 145 million years ago. Its bones had first been discovered almost a hundred years ago not far from Morgan, at a place called Bone Cabin Quarry. Then there was troodon, another meat-eater from the Late Cretaceous 75 million years ago. Because of its large brain, many people thought troodon might have been the most intelligent of the dinosaurs.

Then Fenton had an idea—he could just ask Max's computer program to give him a list of the dinosaurs that were the right height and had lived in the right place. Max Bellman was Fenton's best friend back in New York, and he was a computer genius. Max had designed a computer game called Treasure Quest, which the two boys played long-distance by modem. And when Fenton had first moved to Wyoming, Max had helped him put together a computer program that could look up information on dinosaurs.

"Hey, Dad," said Fenton, "can I go upstairs now? There's something I want to check out on the computer."

"Sure, if you're done with your dinner, son," answered Mr. Rumplemayer.

Fenton pushed back his chair and hurried out of the kitchen and up the stairs to the study on the second floor of the house. He sat down in front of the computer and activated the dinosaur-search program.

The program contained information on all of the dinosaurs listed in Fenton's collection of dinosaur books, including each dinosaur's size, when and where it had lived, whether it had walked on two or four feet, and whether it had been a carnivore, a meat-eater, or a herbivore, a vegetarian. After thinking for a minute, Fenton instructed the program to look up all the dinosaurs that had been less than four feet tall and had lived in western North America.

A few moments later, a long list of dinosaur names appeared on the screen. In addition to the ones Fenton had already thought of, there were many others. Too many, in fact, to be of any real help.

Fenton sighed. The spine bones that had been found at Sleeping Bear could belong to any one of these dinosaurs, he thought, looking at the list. So, until he had some more information on this dinosaur, the computer program wouldn't really be able to help him. At least tomorrow was Saturday, which meant he could get out to the dig site early. Maybe actually seeing the bones themselves would give him some ideas.

Later that night, Fenton lay in bed in his attic bedroom looking at the *Powerboy and Lightning* comic book that Willy had lent him. In this episode, Powerboy and Lightning had to save their town from an evil inventor who was threatening to blow it up with his new mega-bomb. In the end, Lightning ended up risking his life by carrying off the explosive between his teeth.

As Fenton turned the pages of the comic book, he couldn't help thinking of the dog he had seen on his way home from Willy's. It had definitely been a pretty cool dog. It had really seemed to understand him; in fact, it almost seemed smart enough to do some of the stuff that Lightning did. And it was really loyal and determined, too. Fenton was sure that wherever he had thrown that stick the dog would have managed to find it. No doubt about it, it was a pretty amazing dog.

Fenton sighed. He couldn't help imagining what it would be like if the dog was his. But there was no way, he reminded himself. His parents had made it very clear—no dogs. Anyway, at this very moment the dog was probably curled up asleep in someone else's house somewhere.

At least I hope so, thought Fenton, shivering a little as he looked out the window at the cool, dark night.

4

"Well, hello there, Fenton!" called Charlie Smalls, one of the paleontologists working at the dig site. "Are you here to help us dig?"

"You bet," said Fenton, climbing off his bike and walking across the dirt to the large area of rock where Charlie and Mr. Rumplemayer were working. "Where's Professor Martin?"

"Oh, she's back in the trailer, cleaning up those spine bones and finishing her analysis of the rock," said Fenton's father. "You're just in time to help us dig in this new area, son." He indicated a mound of rock that had been partially chipped away to expose the knobby edge of a piece of bone.

"Cool," said Fenton, peering at the fossil. "What is it?"

"I assume it's another piece from the dinosaur," said Mr. Rumplemayer. "But we won't know which piece until we get it uncovered."

"No problem," said Fenton, taking a pick and squatting down next to Charlie and his father. Fenton loved digging for dinosaurs. Since moving to Wyoming, he had already helped out with two important fossil finds.

As Fenton began to scrape away at the rock surrounding the piece of bone, he felt excitement building up inside him. The mystery of what kind of dinosaur had been buried here might even be solved once they got this fossil exposed.

Fenton dug alongside his father and Charlie, using first the larger tools and then the smaller ones to carefully scrape dirt and rock away from the fossil. As more of the bone became exposed, Fenton could see that it was long and narrow, with a flat, foot-shaped knob at one end that almost made it look like some kind of mallet, or a golf club. There were also several small scratchlike indentations on the bone's surface.

"What do you think, Charlie?" asked Mr. Rumplemayer, looking down at the fossil.

"No doubt about it; it's a pubis," said Charlie.

"Wow," said Fenton. He knew that the pubis was one of the three main bones that made up a hip. It could also be an important clue in identifying what group of dinosaurs a particular specimen belonged to.

Every dinosaur was a member of one of two groups: the saurischian, or "reptile-hipped" dinosaurs, and the ornithischian, or "bird-hipped" dinosaurs. Saurischians could be herbivores or carnivores, but ornithischians were always herbivores. There were several ways in which their skeletons differed. One was that the ornithischians had special bones that looked a bit like beaks in front of their teeth. Another was the structure of their hips. An ornithischian pubis was very slender, and it was positioned directly alongside another bone in the hip, called the ischium. A saurischian pubis pointed away from the ischium, and it had a footlike knob at one end.

Fenton looked down at the mallet-shaped bone.

"So this means the dinosaur's a saurischian, right?" he said, pointing to the piece at the end of the fossil.

"It sure looks that way," said Charlie.

"My guess, from the size of this bone and the pieces of the spine we found, is that it might be one of the small, swift saurischian meat-eaters," said Fenton's father.

Like ornitholestes, thought Fenton, or troodon. He tried to remember which of the other dinosaurs on the list the computer had come up with were saurischians.

Just then Professor Martin came walking over from the trailer that the paleontologists used as an office.

"I've finished analyzing that rock sample we took from around the spine bones," she said.

"Oh good," said Fenton's father. "What have you come up with?"

"It appears to be from the Late Cretaceous, I'd say about 75 to 80 million years old," said Professor Martin. "And I've discovered something else, too."

"What's that?" asked Charlie.

"It's bentonite," said Professor Martin.

"What?" asked Fenton.

"Bentonite. It's a volcanic rock."

"Volcanic?" repeated Fenton. "You mean from a volcano?"

"That's right," said Professor Martin. "From an area that was covered by volcanic ash, to be exact."

"Wow," said Fenton. "So that must have been how the dinosaur died and became a fossil."

"It certainly appears that way, son," agreed Fenton's father.

Fenton looked around, imagining the way things must have been back in the Late Cretaceous. A small saurischian dinosaur ran swiftly by, darting among the bushes, unaware of the danger of the smoking volcano nearby. Suddenly there was a rumble beneath the earth, and the volcano began to smoke more furiously. The dinosaur paused. There was a loud roar, and the volcano began to spew forth deadly gas, lava, and clouds of ash. With no chance for escape, the dinosaur quickly suffocated and was buried by the ash.

"Well, well," said Mr. Rumplemayer, cutting into Fenton's thoughts. "A volcano—that's good news for us."

"Bad news for the dinosaur, though," joked Charlie.

"Why is it good news for us, Dad?" asked Fenton.

"It means we're more likely to find a complete fossil here," said his father.

"Ash can do a pretty good job of trapping animals," explained Professor Martin. "Unlike a skeleton that's been exposed to weather or other environmental forces, the skeleton of an animal that's been covered in ash can stay pretty complete."

"I get it," said Fenton. "By trapping the dinosaur, the ash kind of protects the bones and keeps them all together."

That was great news. If most of the dinosaur's bones turned up, there shouldn't be any trouble identifying what kind it had been. Already they knew for sure that it was a saurischian and that it had lived in the Late Cretaceous, which was a lot more than they had known the day before.

Fenton thought about the computer program back at the house. Maybe now, with this additional information, it would be able to tell him more specifically what kind of dinosaur this had been. He couldn't wait to get back home to the computer and see what he could come up with.

5

Fenton coasted on his bicycle down Sleeping Bear Mountain Road, looking out over the town of Morgan spread below him and thinking about the latest fossil find at the dig site. The paleontologists had invited him to stay for lunch, but Fenton had been far too eager to get back to the computer. The new information about the dinosaur should definitely narrow things down, and might even be able to give him the answer. He imagined the looks on the dig team's faces when he announced that he had figured out what kind of dinosaur it had been that had been trapped by the lava.

Just then Fenton thought he heard something peculiar. In addition to the sound of his bicycle gears clicking, there was another sound, a rhythmic tapping, almost like running feet. Slowing down, he glanced over his shoulder. There, running alongside the back wheel of the bike, was the dog from the day before! It trotted along, its tail wagging and its tongue dangling out of one side of its mouth.

Fenton put on his brakes, stopping his bike with a screech. The dog stopped too, and looked up at him, panting.

"Hey, fella, what are you doing here?" asked Fenton.

The dog gazed back up at him and wagged its tail.

Fenton looked around, but there was no one in sight. It was as if the dog had just appeared out of nowhere. Fenton shook his head. This was definitely pretty strange.

The dog cocked its head, and let out a little whine.

"What?" said Fenton, reaching down to scratch its ears. "What is it, fella?"

The dog jumped up onto its hind legs, putting its front paws on Fenton's leg. Taken by surprise, Fenton was thrown off balance. He struggled to stay upright, but the next thing he knew, he had toppled over onto the road, bicycle and all. The dog leapt on him happily, barking and licking his face.

"All right, all right!" said Fenton, laughing and trying to brush the dog off him. He struggled back to his feet and righted his bicycle.

The dog looked at Fenton and barked, wagging its tail.

"What is it?" asked Fenton. "Hey, don't you have a home, fella?"

The dog sat down in the road, cocked its head to one side, and let out a low whimper, almost as if it had understood Fenton's question.

Right then Fenton made a decision. He had to find some way to adopt this dog. It was pretty obvious that it didn't belong to anyone; not only was it running around completely on its own for the second day in a row, but it wasn't wearing a collar. It couldn't belong to anyone; in fact, it seemed to think it belonged to *him.*

"I guess I'd better give you a name," said Fenton.

The dog looked at him expectantly.

Fenton thought a moment. This was obviously a pretty amazing dog, and it deserved a really good name. Maybe he should name it after someone—someone really smart. He tried to think of some names of people he admired. There was Dr. Gideon Mantell, a British doctor who had identified the first dinosaur teeth over a hundred and seventy years ago. But Gideon was sort of a weird name for a dog. Then Fenton thought of Sir Richard Owen, the scientist who had first recognized the fact that dinosaurs belonged in their own special group, that they were different from lizards or any other animals. Owen had even invented the word "dinosaur."

"That's it," said Fenton. "How about Owen?"

The dog looked at him and barked once in answer.

"Okay," said Fenton, laughing. "From now on, you're Owen." He put out his hand, and Owen licked it. "Good boy. Good dog, Owen."

But there was still one big problem. Fenton knew that there was no way his father was going to let him have a dog. But he also knew that he couldn't just leave Owen out here alone, either.

Hey, maybe Willy will have a good idea, thought Fenton. Maybe I can even keep Owen at his house.

"Okay, come on, Owen," said Fenton, climbing back onto his bike.

Owen stood up, wagging his tail.

Fenton rode the rest of the way down the mountain, Owen trotting happily behind him. They reached the turnoff for Fenton's and Willy's houses, and Fenton followed the fork to the right, toward the Whitefoxes'.

"Willy! Willy! Are you there?" called Fenton as he rode up Willy's driveway, with Owen close behind him.

"Oh, hello, Fenton, is that you?" asked Willy's mother through the screen door.

"Hi, Mrs. Whitefox." Fenton leaned his bike against the house and reaching down to pat Owen on the head. "Is Willy around?"

"Sure, just a moment," she said. "Willy! Fenton's here!"

Just then the screen door burst open, and Jane came rushing out with Simonetta in her arms.

"Hi, Fenkon!" she called happily. "I heard you talking out here and I—"

She spotted Owen, and her eyes opened wide.

"Oh, no!" she shrieked. "What's that?"

Owen looked up at her and started to bark.

"Aaah!" she yelled, holding Simonetta high above her head. Owen must have thought she wanted to play, because he leapt up and began jumping around her, barking.

"Help! Help!" cried Jane, still holding the kitten above her head. "Fenkon, do something!"

"Down, boy!" called Fenton. "Owen, stop that!" He tried to grab the dog. But without a collar, Owen was hard to hold on to, and he kept slipping through Fenton's grasp.

Willy pushed open the screen door.

"Cool!" he said, standing in the doorway and looking at the scene appreciatively. "A dog!"

Jane hurried over to the door, stopping to give Fenton a teary look.

"Fenkon, how could you!" she said, pushing past Willy to get inside.

Fenton threw both his arms around the dog's neck.

"I told you to stop!" he said sternly, putting his face close to the dog's. "Bad dog! Bad Owen!"

Owen sat down and gave Fenton a guilty look. Then he licked Fenton's face. Fenton grinned.

"Wow," said Willy. "Where'd you get the dog?"

"Actually, it was more like *he* got *me*," joked Fenton. He told Willy about the way Owen had first shown up near the shack the day before, and then again on the road today. "I named him Owen," he finished.

"That's a pretty cool story," said Willy, bending down to pet Owen.

"He's a pretty cool dog," said Fenton. He looked around

33

for a stick. "Watch this." Fenton lifted the stick above his head. "Okay, boy, ready?"

Owen leapt to his feet and started to bark.

"Okay, fella, go get it," said Fenton, throwing the stick into the woods behind Willy's house.

"Forget it. He'll never be able to find it," said Willy as Owen bounded off.

"Just wait," said Fenton.

Sure enough, a few moments later Owen appeared from out of the trees, waving the stick proudly in his mouth.

"Good, boy! Good dog, Owen!" said Fenton as Owen brought him the stick.

"Hey, can I try?" asked Willy.

"Sure," said Fenton, handing him the stick.

"Okay, go get it, Owen," said Willy, throwing the stick.

Once again, a few moments later Owen appeared from out of the woods with the stick in his mouth. He trotted toward Fenton.

"No, Owen, bring it to Willy," said Fenton.

The dog stopped and looked around.

"To *Willy*," Fenton said again, pointing.

Owen bounded toward Willy, wagging his tail.

"Hey, that's pretty good," said Willy, reaching down to take the stick from Owen. "It's almost like he understood what you said."

"I know," said Fenton proudly. "Hey, toss me the stick. Let's see if he'll do it again."

Willy threw Fenton the stick, and Owen ran after it, barking happily.

"Okay, Owen," said Fenton, handing the dog the stick. "Now bring it to *Willy*."

Owen took the stick in his mouth and trotted over to Willy.

"Wow, Fenton," said Willy. "That's some great dog you've got."

"I know," said Fenton. "There's only one problem with him."

"What's that?" asked Willy.

"I can't keep him," said Fenton.

"Why not?" asked Willy. "He doesn't belong to anyone else, right? I mean, he's not wearing a collar, and he did try to follow you home twice."

"I know," said Fenton, "but my father will never let me have a dog. Believe me, I know. Back in New York I must have asked my parents for a dog about a million times, and they always said no, that a dog was too much responsibility. Finally I just stopped asking."

"Gee, that's too bad," said Willy.

"I know," said Fenton, scratching Owen behind the ears. He looked at Willy. "Listen, I was thinking. Maybe I could keep him here, at your house."

"No way," said Willy, shaking his head. "Didn't you see the way he was acting with Simonetta? Cats and dogs just don't mix, Fenton. Besides, my dad's allergic to dogs."

"Oh," said Fenton, disappointed. Now what was he going to do with Owen?

"Hey, I've got an idea," said Willy. "What about Maggie? There's lots of room on the ranch; maybe he can stay with her."

"I guess that could work," said Fenton. He had kind of liked the idea of having Owen right next door at Willy's, but he knew that the important thing was just to find the dog a good home. Besides, he could always go visit Owen at Maggie's.

"Let's give her a call," said Willy. "On second thought, maybe you'd better wait out here with Owen. I'll go inside and call her."

"Okay," said Fenton.

Fenton sat down on Willy's back step, and Owen lay down beside him. Owen turned over on his back, and Fenton rubbed his belly.

A few minutes later, Willy appeared at the door again.

"Maggie says to come on over," he said.

"Wow, really?" said Fenton. "So it's okay?"

"She says it should be fine," said Willy. "They already have a bunch of dogs on the ranch, so one more probably won't make too much of a difference."

Fenton looked at Owen. He still couldn't help wishing that Owen could stay with him, at his house.

"Okay," said Fenton, standing up. "Let's go."

Fifteen minutes later, Fenton and Willy were riding up Sleeping Bear Mountain Road to the Carr horse ranch, with Owen trotting happily behind them. Fenton looked around, amazed, as they rode along the split-rail fence that divided the Carrs' property from the road. It was still hard for him to believe that one family really owned all that land. Fenton had been friends with Maggie for only a little while, and although he had ridden by the ranch many times on his bicycle and seen the horses grazing behind the fence, he had never actually been on the ranch.

The rolling fields seemed to stretch for miles in every direction as Fenton and Willy rode through the big metal gates emblazoned with horseshoes turned on their sides to look like Cs. In the distance was a sprawling, one-story white house and several other large buildings.

"Maggie said to meet her near the stable," said Willy, heading toward one of the large buildings.

"Okay," said Fenton, pedaling after him. He was glad Willy was there. On his own, he was sure he wouldn't have been able to tell which building was the stable.

As they rode closer to the building, Fenton spotted Maggie standing in front of it. She waved.

"Hi," she said as Fenton and Willy pulled up in front of her on their bikes. She looked down at Owen. "So this is him, huh?"

"Yeah," said Fenton. "His name's Owen."

"Hi, Owen," said Maggie, putting out her hand. Owen sniffed it and wagged his tail.

"So is it really all right if he stays here?" asked Fenton.

Maggie shrugged. "Why not? There's already a bunch of other dogs that run around on the ranch and sleep here in the stables with the horses. No one'll even notice if there's one more."

"You mean he has to stay out here?" said Fenton.

"Sure," said Maggie. "All the dogs stay out here."

"Gee," said Fenton, looking down at Owen. "I was kind of hoping that he could stay in the house with you."

"Are you kidding?" said Maggie. "There's no way my mother would ever let any of the dogs in the house. She'd be way too afraid they'd mess up some of her precious antique furniture or something."

"Oh," said Fenton, disappointed.

"Don't worry, Fen. He'll be okay," said Maggie. "He'll have plenty of other dogs to keep him company."

"I guess," said Fenton, looking at Owen. But he couldn't help thinking that Owen would be happier inside, where he could be with people.

"Where'd you get this dog, anyway, Fen?" asked Maggie.

"Nowhere, really," said Fenton. "I mean, I first saw him when he tried to follow me home from Willy's yesterday."

"Really?" said Maggie. "That's kind of neat."

"And then he showed up again when Fenton was on his way back from the dig site today," said Willy.

"Oh, that reminds me," said Fenton. "My father and the others have uncovered some cool bones out at Sleeping Bear. They think they're from a dinosaur that was caught in the ash from a volcano."

"Wow," said Willy.

"What kind of dinosaur is it, Fen?" asked Maggie.

"They're not sure yet," said Fenton. "But they do know that it was some kind of saurischian from the late Cretaceous, and that it probably stood about waist-high to a grown-up. It may have been one of the smaller saurischian meat-eaters."

"That information sounds like a pretty good start," said Maggie.

"Yeah," said Willy. "I'm sure they'll be able to figure out what kind of dinosaur it was."

"Actually, my father and the others may have that answer sooner than they think," said Fenton, grinning.

"What do you mean?" asked Willy.

"Well, I was just heading home to do a little research on the computer," said Fenton.

"Oh, you mean that dinosaur program you told me about that your friend in New York designed?" asked Maggie.

"Exactly," said Fenton. "I tried to use it last night when my father first told me about the fossil find, but I couldn't get a definite answer. I'm hoping the new information I got today will help."

"Cool," said Maggie.

"Hey, do you guys want to come over?" asked Fenton. "We can all try the computer program together."

"Okay," said Willy.

"Great," said Maggie. "Let me just go get my bike."

Fenton looked down at Owen, who was looking back at him and wagging his tail expectantly.

"Sorry, boy," said Fenton, taking a deep breath and trying not to notice how sad he suddenly felt. "You can't come with me. From now on, this is going to have to be your home."

6

"Okay," said Fenton, stacking the roast-beef sandwiches he had just made on a plate. "You guys bring the juice and the cookies, all right?"

"No problem," said Maggie, picking up the bag of cookies and popping one of them in her mouth.

Willy grabbed the juice glasses, and he and Maggie followed Fenton up the stairs.

"Okay," said Fenton, "time to try the dinosaur program."

"So we can find out what kind of dinosaur it is, right?" asked Willy.

"Let's hope so," said Fenton as they walked into the study. "I'll just tell the computer to look for any saurischian dinosaur that lived in western North America in the Late Cretaceous and that stood under four feet tall."

"Wow," said Maggie. "This must be some program. I guess your friend in New York knows a lot about computers."

"Max is a computer genius," said Fenton proudly. He sat down in front of the computer. "Now, first we input the information we have" — he typed in several commands on the keyboard —"and then we ask the computer to search." He pressed a few more keys.

"And that's it?" said Willy, chewing on his sandwich.

"That's it," said Fenton. "Here it comes."

They all leaned closer to the computer, to see the answer. A list of dinosaurs appeared on the screen.

"Oh," said Fenton, disappointed. The list was shorter than the first list had been, but it was still too long to be useful.

"I don't get it," said Willy. "Which of those dinosaurs is it?"

"That's just the problem," said Fenton, sighing. "We can't tell."

"Gee, I guess we need even more information in order to find the answer," said Maggie.

"Yeah," said Fenton. "I guess so." He thought a moment. "I've got an idea. Why don't we go out to the dig site tomorrow? Maybe if we all put our heads together, we can come up with something."

Later that evening, Fenton sat in front of the computer and activated the modem. It was eight o'clock—time for his weekly game of Treasure Quest with Max in New York.

]HI MAX ITS ME[

Fenton keyed in.

<HI FENTON. HOWS IT GOING>

43

came Max's response.

]OK I GUESS. I FOUND A DOG BUT I CANT KEEP HIM[

<2 BAD. MY MOM MIGHT LET ME GET A SNAKE>

]REALLY?[

<WELL, SHE SAID NO, BUT IM WORKING ON HER. HOWS THE DIG SITE?>

]GOOD. THERE R SOME NEW BONES FROM A DINO THAT WAS KILLED BY A VOLCANO[

<NEAT. WHAT KIND OF DINO?>

]NO ONE KNOWS YET. I TRIED 2 USE THE PROGRAM U DESIGNED 2 FIND OUT, BUT IT WOULDNT TELL ME[

<Y NOT?>

]I DIDNT HAVE ENOUGH INFORMATION ABOUT THE DINOSAUR, SO THE LIST IT GAVE ME WAS REALLY LONG[

<OK THAT MAKES SENSE. I THOUGHT U WERE TRYING TO SAY THERES SOMETHING WRONG WITH THE PROGRAM, WHICH IS IMPOSSIBLE. WANT TO PLAY TQ NOW?>

]OK[

typed Fenton.

For the next forty-five minutes the boys were completely involved in playing Treasure Quest. And for the first time all day, Fenton didn't have a single thought about the dinosaur at the dig site, or about Owen, either.

7

The next day Fenton stood in front of the refrigerator, looking for something to give Maggie for Owen. He missed Owen, and it made him feel better to think of sending him a treat of some kind. It was definitely time to do some food shopping, though; he, Willy, and Maggie had finished the last of the bread and the roast beef yesterday, and there wasn't much else in the refrigerator.

Olives? No, dogs probably weren't too fond of olives. A lemon? Not much he could do with that. And the mayonnaise and ketchup wouldn't be much good either.

Fenton moved to the cupboards. There were two boxes of cereal, a box of spaghetti, and the rest of the bag of cookies. Cookies, thought Fenton. He put some in his jean-jacket pocket.

Just then he heard Willy's voice from outside.

"Fenton! Fenton, you ready?"

"Sure, Willy!" Fenton called back. "Just a minute!"

He picked his triceratops baseball cap up off the kitchen table and jammed it backward onto his head.

"Hi," he said, bounding into the backyard.

"Hi," said Willy. "We're going out to Sleeping Bear, right?"

"Yeah," said Fenton. "Maggie said she'd meet us on the road in front of her place."

Ten minutes later they rode their bikes up to the gate of the Carr Ranch, where Maggie was waiting with her bicycle.

"Fen, I have some bad news," she said as Fenton and Willy pulled their bikes up alongside her.

"What is it?" asked Fenton.

"It's Owen," said Maggie.

"Oh, no!" said Fenton. "What happened? Is he all right?"

"He's fine," said Maggie. "But I don't really think it's going to work out. I don't know if he can stay at the ranch anymore."

"Why not?" asked Willy.

"Did he do something?" asked Fenton.

"No, it's not really Owen's fault," Maggie explained. "It's the other dogs. You see, they all grew up on the ranch together, and they all know each other really well. Owen's sort of like an outsider to them, and I guess they feel threatened."

"You mean they don't get along with him?" asked Fenton.

"Not at all," said Maggie, shaking her head. "In fact, it got so bad that I had to take him into the house."

"But what about your mother?" asked Willy.

"She doesn't know," said Maggie. "I sneaked him inside early this morning and put him in the back storeroom. My mother never goes there. But he definitely can't stay too long;

someone's bound to find him eventually. I'm afraid you're going to have to take him back, Fen."

"But how can I?" asked Fenton. "What am I going to do with him?"

"Beats me," said Maggie. "But I do know he can't stay at my house much longer."

"All right," said Fenton. "Give me a day or two to come up with something, though, okay?"

"Sure," said Maggie. "I guess I can keep him hidden for a while longer."

"Oh, and give him these, would you?" Fenton reached into his jean-jacket pocket and pulled out the cookies.

"Cookies?" said Willy. "For a dog?"

"They were all I could find," said Fenton. "I thought he might be getting hungry."

"Don't worry, Fen," said Maggie. "Owen'll eat like a king while he's with me."

"What do you mean?" asked Fenton.

"I'll just ask Dina for whatever I think he might like," said Maggie.

"Oh, right," said Fenton. Dina was Maggie's family's cook. Maggie had told Fenton that all she had to do was walk into the kitchen and ask for something and Dina would make it for her.

Maggie laughed. "Won't Dina be surprised when I tell her I'm really in the mood for an old steak bone and some dog biscuits!"

Fenton and Willy laughed too.

"Hey, speaking of bones," said Fenton, "let's get out to the dig site and check out those fossils."

"Hey, where is everybody?" asked Fenton as he, Maggie, and Willy climbed off their bikes near the fossil excavation site.

He looked around, but his father, Charlie, and Professor Martin were nowhere in sight.

"Dad?" he called. He looked at Maggie and Willy. "Maybe they're in the trailer."

"Gee," said Willy, walking over to the rock where Fenton had worked with his father and Charlie, "look at all this stuff!"

Fenton hurried over to see what Willy was talking about. There, still partly embedded in the rock, was the hip bone that he had helped dig up. Nearby were several other pieces of bone that Fenton hadn't seen before. Lying beside them was the straw hat that Professor Martin usually wore.

"Wow, I guess they must have just found these," said Fenton, surveying the fossils.

Maggie walked over and stood beside him. "What are they?"

Fenton pointed to the pubis. "Well, that's a bone from the hip that I helped uncover, but these other fossils are new." He bent down to look at several squarish chunks of bone arranged in a slightly curved line. "I'm not absolutely sure, but these look a lot like they could be part of the dinosaur's neck."

"Neat," said Willy.

Fenton moved over to examine another group of bone fragments nearby. The pieces were rather small, and it was pretty hard to tell what part of the animal they might be from. Then he spotted a long, narrow bone segment with several small, triangular pieces arranged along one side of it. Suddenly he realized what he was looking at.

"Teeth!" he said excitedly.

"Really?" asked Maggie. "Where?"

"Right there," said Fenton, pointing to the triangular pieces protruding from the bone. "I guess this must be a piece of the dinosaur's jaw."

Fenton wondered if these new bones had finally made it possible for his father and the team to identify the dinosaur. Although he was eager to have the mystery solved, Fenton couldn't help feeling a little disappointed at the idea that he might not get a chance to come up with the answer himself.

"Wow," said Willy. "Those teeth look pretty fierce."

Just then Fenton heard Professor Martin's voice .

"Hello, everyone," she said.

"Hi, Professor Martin," said Fenton. "Hey, where are my dad and Charlie?"

"They're over behind the trailer. I just came back here to get my hat," she said. "We've been having a rather frustrating morning over here, so we decided to break early for lunch."

"Frustrating? What do you mean?" asked Fenton. He

pointed to the new fossils. "It looks to me like you've had a great morning."

"Really," agreed Maggie. "It seems like you've made some pretty important finds."

"That's for sure," said Willy.

"It's more like we've made some *confusing* finds," said Professor Martin, sighing.

"Huh?" said Fenton. "It all seems pretty clear to me."

"Fenton thinks those bones over there are from the dinosaur's neck," said Willy.

"Yes, they are," said Professor Martin. "And there's no problem with those. What has us stumped is this other piece, the one from the jawbone."

"How so?" asked Maggie.

"Yeah, what's wrong with it?" asked Fenton.

"Well," said Professor Martin, "did you take a close look?"

"No, not really," said Fenton. The truth was, he had been so excited by the new finds that he hadn't had time to examine them very closely.

Fenton crouched down over the jawbone. It was long and slender, with a larger, curved chunk at one end. He could see a bunch of little indentations in its surface, almost like scratch marks. In addition, there were several teeth sticking out of the bone. The teeth were triangular, and slightly curved, with a row of tiny points running along their edges.

"Hey!" said Fenton, looking at the rows of points again.

"Those aren't carnivore teeth." Fenton knew that only herbivore dinosaurs had teeth like that; they used the jagged edges of their teeth to grind up plants. Meat-eating dinosaurs had smooth, crescent-shaped, pointy teeth, with serrations or grooves like steak knives.

"That's right," said Professor Martin.

"But I thought you said the dinosaur was a meat-eater, Fenton," said Willy.

"That's what my dad thought," said Fenton.

"And indeed," said Professor Martin, "most of the smaller saurischians from the Late Cretaceous that lived in this area were carnivores. But that's not the real problem here."

"Really," said Maggie. "Maybe this dinosaur was just one of the herbivorous saurischians."

Fenton glanced back at the fossil. Suddenly, he saw exactly what was wrong with it. There, at the end of the jawbone, in front of the teeth, was a large, curved chunk of bone that looked almost like a beak.

"Wait a minute," said Fenton, amazed by what he saw. He pointed to the beaklike bone. "What's that doing there?"

"Exactly," said Professor Martin.

"What?" said Willy. "I don't get it."

"That piece of bone in front of the teeth," said Fenton. "Saurischians never have those. Only ornithischian dinosaurs have them."

"So then maybe it's an ornithischian," said Maggie.

Fenton shook his head. "No way. That piece of the hip I helped uncover could only belong to a saurischian."

"But how can that be?" asked Maggie.

"It doesn't make any sense," said Willy.

"That's right," said Professor Martin. "And now you know why we've all been so frustrated by this find. There just doesn't seem to be any explanation. We were really hoping to come up with some answers, but now the identity of this dinosaur is more of a mystery than ever." She sighed. "For all we know, it may never be solved."

Not if I can help it, thought Fenton. He knew that the mystery of the dinosaur's identity would be more of a challenge than ever now, but he was also more determined than ever to solve it.

8

"I don't know, Fenton. I just can't seem to make any sense of it at all," said Mr. Rumplemayer as the two of them stood in front of the kitchen sink that night, washing and drying the dinner dishes.

"It's definitely pretty strange," said Fenton, taking the wet plate his father had handed him and wiping it dry with a dishcloth. "I mean, what kind of dinosaur could have an ornithischian mouth and a saurischian hip bone?"

"It breaks all the rules we know about dinosaurs," agreed his father, rinsing a pot and handing it to Fenton. "It's a shame, too, especially since we were expecting this to be quite an impressive fossil find."

"Because of the volcanic ash?" said Fenton, wiping the pot dry with his cloth.

"That's right," said Mr. Rumplemayer. "You know, we were all very excited at first when we discovered those bones from the neck and jaw. We were hoping it would be an important clue to the dinosaur's identity. But it seems to have just made things more confusing."

Just then the telephone rang.

"I'll get it," said Fenton, putting down his dishcloth and heading over to the yellow telephone mounted on the wall above the counter. "Hello?"

"Hi, Fen. It's me."

"Maggie?" asked Fenton.

"That's right," she said. "Listen, I have to talk to you about Owen."

"Oh?" said Fenton, glancing toward his father.

"Yeah," said Maggie. "I'm sorry, but he just can't stay here anymore."

"But you said you'd give me a couple of days, Maggie," said Fenton, his eyes still on his father. "What's going on? What's wrong?"

"Well, for starters, he made a total mess of the storage room," said Maggie. "He dragged all this stuff off of shelves and out of boxes and pulled it into this little closet where I had put a blanket for him to sleep on. And then he chewed everything to bits! You should see the place—he got at my old swim fins, and my sister Lila's tennis racket, and this straw hat with flowers on it that my mother wears every Easter, and a bunch of other stuff."

"Gee, Maggie," said Fenton, "that's terrible."

"I'll say," said Maggie. "Lila will be fit to kill when she sees her tennis racket."

"I'm really sorry about this, Maggie," said Fenton.

Maggie sighed. "It's not your fault, Fen. I know Owen's just following his natural instincts. Dogs chew things. But he definitely can't stay here any longer. You're going to have to take him back."

"Okay, okay," said Fenton. He glanced at his father and lowered his voice. "Listen, just bring him over here before school tomorrow, okay? But wait till my father leaves for work. I'll put the flag up on our mailbox once he's gone so you know the coast is clear."

"Okay," said Maggie. "See you then."

"Bye," said Fenton, hanging up.

Fenton's father finished washing the last of the dishes and turned off the water. "What was that all about, son?"

"Uh, what do you mean?" asked Fenton nervously.

"Oh, it just sounded like Maggie was having some kind of problem, that's all," said his father.

"Problem?" repeated Fenton, his mind racing.

"Well, yes," said his father. "It certainly seemed that way."

"Oh, it's nothing, really," said Fenton. Then he thought of something. "Actually, she's just frustrated that no one can figure out what's going on with that dinosaur you found up at the dig site."

"She is?" said Mr. Rumplemayer, raising his eyebrows. "I had no idea it meant so much to her."

"Oh, sure," said Fenton. "Maggie's into it. Listen, Dad, can I go up to my room now? I kind of have some really important homework I need to do."

"Why, certainly, son," said Mr. Rumplemayer. "Don't let me keep you from your schoolwork."

"Okay, see you later, Dad," said Fenton, hurrying out of the kitchen.

Whew, he thought as he hurried out of the kitchen and climbed the stairs, that had been kind of tough. But it was still nothing compared to how tough it would be to figure out what he was going to do with Owen.

9

The next morning, Fenton and Willy hid with their bicycles in the bushes along Sleeping Bear Mountain Road.

"Gosh, your dad better leave soon," said Willy. "We don't have that much time before school starts."

"I know," said Fenton, looking at his watch. "Wait, I think I hear him coming."

There was the rumble of an engine in the distance. Fenton and Willy crouched lower in the bushes as it grew closer.

"That's him," said Fenton, as the green pickup truck drove past them toward the mountain. "Okay, come on, let's get back to the house and wait for Maggie."

They pulled their bikes out of the bushes and climbed onto them.

"Hang on a sec," said Fenton, stopping his bike at the cluster of mailboxes by the turnoff for his and Willy's houses. He flipped the red flag on his mailbox to the vertical position.

"What's that for?" asked Willy. "Are you going to mail a letter?"

"It's a signal," explained Fenton. "For Maggie, so she'll know the coast is clear."

"Oh," said Willy. "I get it."

The two boys rode up Fenton's driveway, leaned their bikes against the garage, and sat down on the porch steps.

"Maggie should be here any minute," said Fenton.

"Good," said Willy. "Then maybe we can still get to school before the bell rings."

But ten minutes went by, and there was still no sign of Maggie.

"I don't understand it," said Fenton. "I told her to meet us here."

"If she takes any longer, we're definitely going to get demerits," said Willy.

"Yeah," said Fenton. "I guess you're right." The teachers at Morgan Elementary gave out demerits to kids who broke the rules. Four demerits and you had to stay after school for detention. So far, Fenton hadn't gotten any.

Just then Fenton heard rustling in the bushes nearby.

"Fen?" whispered a voice. "Fen? Is it okay?"

"Maggie?" said Fenton, peering into the bushes. "Is that you?"

"Yeah," the voice whispered. "Can we come out?"

"Sure," said Fenton. "What are you doing in there anyway?"

"Really," said Willy. "We've been waiting for you forever."

"*You've* been waiting for *me*?" said Maggie indignantly, stepping out of the bushes with Owen. In one hand she held a rope that was attached to Owen's neck, and the other hand was muzzling Owen's mouth. She let go of his mouth and he began to bark loudly and strain at the rope. "I've been riding my bike back and forth in front of your mailbox for ages, waiting for the signal."

"What are you talking about?" said Fenton, raising his voice over Owen's barking. "I put the flag up."

"Yeah," said Willy. "I saw Fenton do it."

"Well, it's not up now," said Maggie.

"That's weird," said Fenton.

"Oh, I know," said Willy. "I bet the mailman put it down."

"The mailman?" said Fenton.

"Sure," said Willy. "He drives by in the mornings to pick up the mail. He probably saw the flag up and stopped, thinking you had a letter in there. When the mailbox was empty, he must have figured it was a mistake and put the flag down."

"Gee," said Fenton, "so much for that signal."

"Well, whatever," said Maggie. "All I know is I've been riding by for the past fifteen minutes. Finally, I decided to sneak up here and see what was going on. Let me tell you, it

61

wasn't easy keeping Owen quiet."

"Hi, Owen," said Fenton, looking down at the dog, who was still straining at the rope. He bent down, and Owen began to lick his face happily.

"Here you go, Fen," said Maggie, handing Fenton the rope. "He's all yours."

"What are you going to do with him, Fenton?" asked Willy.

"I don't really know," said Fenton. "I could put him in the house, I guess. . . ."

"I have an idea," said Maggie. "What about the shack?"

"Good thinking," said Fenton. "Is it okay with you, Willy?"

"Sure," said Willy. "Why not?"

"Come on, Owen," said Fenton. "We're going to take you to your new home."

"Yeah," sighed Willy. "And then we're all going to school to get demerits."

Fenton knew Willy was probably right. There was no way they'd get to school on time now. But as he looked at Owen prancing happily alongside him, somehow he didn't even really mind.

"Oh, no!" said Fenton, as he walked into the shack later that afternoon. "Owen, what did you do?"

Owen wagged his tail happily.

"Bad boy," said Fenton, surveying the mess. "Bad dog!"

But Owen sat down and looked guiltily up at Fenton. Then he walked over to the corner, sniffed at a couple of the chewed-up comic books, and barked once.

"Gosh," said Fenton, squatting down to examine what was left of *Monster Mania*. The comic, along with several others, had been dragged into a corner and chewed to pieces.

Just then Fenton heard Willy's voice from outside.

"Fenton? Are you in there?"

"Uh, yes!" Fenton called back. What was he going to tell Willy? For the first time, some of what his parents had always said about how much responsibility was involved in owning a dog was beginning to make sense.

"Hey, Fenton, how's it going?" said Willy, pushing open the door of the shack.

"Um, hi, Willy," said Fenton, glancing guiltily at the pile of comic book scraps in the corner.

"Hey, what's all that?" said Willy, following Fenton's gaze. "Oh, no! My comics!"

"I'm really sorry about this, Willy," Fenton said quickly. "I mean, I'm sure Owen didn't mean any harm."

"Oh, wow," said Willy, crouching down in the corner and examining the shreds of paper. He shook his head. "These are ruined."

"I'm sorry," Fenton said again. "Hey, maybe I can get you some new comic books, Willy."

Willy didn't answer; he just looked sadly down at the pile of paper.

"Owen didn't mean it," said Fenton. "Dogs chew things; Maggie says he's just following his natural instincts."

Owen barked once as if in agreement.

"Yeah, well, I wish he could have followed them somewhere else," said Willy. He fingered the scraps. "Actually, this isn't really so terrible. I mean, it's definitely too bad that he got at my *Monster Mania*—it's one of my favorites—but I think I know where I can get another one. Most of these others weren't that good, anyway, though."

Fenton sighed in relief. "I'm glad you're not too upset."

Willy looked at him.

"Owen definitely can't stay here any longer, though, Fenton," he said. "I'm sorry, but if he does, he'll chew everything in sight."

Fenton looked down at Owen, who had begun to gnaw happily on the Frisbee that Willy had brought out to the shack a few days ago.

"No kidding," said Fenton, shaking his head. "Give me that, Owen." Owen dropped the Frisbee. "Gee, I hope he didn't ruin this, too."

Fenton examined the Frisbee. It looked okay, except for several bite marks in its surface.

"Sorry, Willy," he said, tossing Willy the Frisbee. Then he

64

thought of something. "Hey, let me see that a minute."

Willy threw the Frisbee back to Fenton. Owen must have thought they were playing with him, because he jumped up and tried to get at it.

"Down, Owen," said Fenton, examining the Frisbee closely.

"What is it?" asked Willy. "What's going on?"

"I'm not sure," said Fenton. "It's just . . ." Something about the chewed Frisbee seemed very familiar to Fenton, but he couldn't figure out why. "It's nothing, I guess." He threw the Frisbee back to Willy, and Owen leapt in the air, trying to get at it.

"Well," said Fenton, taking hold of Owen's rope. "I guess I'd better take Owen outside and tie him to a tree or something."

"Will he be okay?" asked Willy.

Fenton shrugged. "I hope so. There's not really much else I can do right now."

"Hey, I'm sorry, Fenton," said Willy. "It's just, if he stays here . . ."

"I know," said Fenton. He pulled on Owen's rope. "Come on, boy, let's go."

Five minutes later, he had secured Owen's rope to a tree about halfway between the shack and his house. Next he went home and got a blanket, a bowl of water, and some cookies, and put them down on the ground.

"I guess I'll have to get you some dog food soon," he said, watching Owen settle down on the blanket and begin to crunch the cookies between his teeth.

As Fenton looked down into Owen's big brown eyes, he couldn't help feeling kind of bad about tying him up outside like this. But there are plenty of trees around for shelter, he reminded himself, and Owen has a blanket to keep warm. It probably wouldn't be too bad. Besides, right now, Fenton didn't really have any other choice.

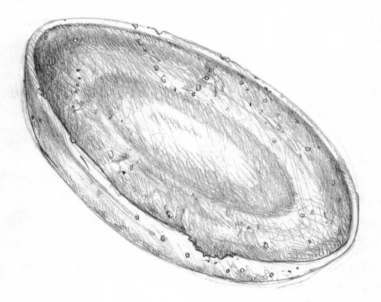

10

Later that afternoon, Fenton pedaled up Sleeping Bear Mountain Road, his latest dinosaur sketchbook and his drawing pencils strapped securely to the rack of his bicycle. He had decided to make some sketches of the bones out at the dig site. Fenton had been drawing dinosaurs practically as long as he could remember, and he had already filled several books with sketches he had made back at the Museum of Natural History, in New York City. Drawing dinosaurs always helped him to understand them better, so, since moving to Morgan, he often brought his sketchbook out to the dig site to make drawings of the fossil finds.

As he rode across the dirt to the excavation site, he could see his father, Charlie, and Professor Martin crouched down over the rock at work.

"Hi, everybody," he said, climbing off his bike, unstrapping his sketchbook and pencils from the rack, and walking toward the excavation site.

"Oh, hello, son," said Mr. Rumplemayer, looking up briefly from the rock. "We haven't really had any more luck here, if that's what you came to find out."

"Yeah," said Charlie, taking off his big cowboy hat and wiping his forehead. "Things are still about as clear as a pond after a mud slide."

"It's certainly very frustrating," agreed Professor Martin, wiping her hands on her pants. "Right now the best we can hope for is to just get these fossils cleaned up and sent off to the museum."

"You mean so they can display them?" asked Fenton. He loved to think of the fossils that he helped to uncover on display back at the museum in New York.

"Well, unfortunately, since we haven't been able to identify which dinosaur they're from, they probably won't be put on display," said Fenton's father. "More likely the museum will just keep them somewhere in storage until someone someday can figure out what they are."

"*If* anyone can ever figure out what they are," said Charlie.

"Well, what do you say we call it a day?" said Mr. Rumplemayer. "Fenton, I'm sorry, but if you came out here to help us dig, you're a little late."

"Actually, I thought I might make some sketches," said Fenton, holding up his notebook.

"Sure, son. Go ahead," said his father. "We've got a few

minutes. I'm going to go back to the trailer and make some notes before I head home."

"I think I'll join you," said Charlie. "I could use a cool drink about now."

"Sounds wonderful," said Professor Martin, standing up and taking off her hat.

As his father and the others made their way toward the trailer, Fenton walked over to where the dinosaur's hip bone lay. He sat down, opened his sketchbook, and took out his pencils.

Once again Fenton noticed the tiny scratchlike indentations on the bone's surface. He decided to include them in his sketch. After all, it was important to record every detail of the fossil.

After finishing his drawing of the pubis, Fenton made his way over to the dinosaur's jawbone. He bent down, peered at the bone, and ran his finger along it. The surface felt rough, and Fenton looked more closely at the fossil. There was no doubt about it; the narrow, scratchlike marks in its surface were exactly like the ones on the pubis.

I wonder if these could turn out to be important? thought Fenton. Then he had an idea. He hurried over to the curved line of bones that had come from the dinosaur's neck. He hadn't examined these bones very carefully the last time he had been out at the dig site, but now he wasn't too surprised to see that these bones too had some of the same marks.

Quickly Fenton drew the jawbone and the neck bones, being careful to copy the scratch marks on each exactly.

Now, he said to himself, what I really need to do is to get a look at those spine bones. He remembered his father saying that Professor Martin had been analyzing a piece of rock from the bones a few days ago. They must still be in the trailer. He picked up his sketchbook and walked over toward it.

Charlie and Professor Martin were sitting outside on folding chairs, drinking sodas. Charlie's feet were resting on a red beverage cooler, and Professor Martin was fanning herself with her hat.

"Hi, there, Fenton," said Charlie. "Would you like a cold soda?"

"No thanks, Charlie," Fenton answered.

"Oh my," said Professor Martin. "Somehow I always get so warm when we're digging. Thank goodness now that autumn's here, the nights have a bit of a chill to them."

At this, Fenton couldn't help thinking of poor Owen, who would be spending the night outside. He hoped it wouldn't be *too* chilly.

Just then Fenton's father came out of the trailer.

"I think I'll have one of those sodas, now, Charlie," he said, sitting down on a rock. "It's been another long day."

Charlie leaned forward and opened the cooler. He tossed a can of soda to Fenton's father.

"Thanks," said Mr. Rumplemayer. He looked at Fenton. "Well, son, did you finish those drawings you wanted to do?"

"Yeah," said Fenton.

"Let's have a look," said Charlie, reaching out his hand.

"Uh, maybe some other time," said Fenton, tucking his sketchbook under his arm. Somehow he didn't feel like showing the sketches to anyone until he was sure what the scratch marks were. "Right now I kind of want to take a look at those spine bones, if that's okay."

"Sure," said Charlie. "I understand."

"Go right ahead," said Professor Martin. "They're inside, on the table."

Fenton pulled open the door to the trailer and stepped inside. As usual, the trailer was completely cluttered; books and papers were crammed onto the rickety metal shelves against one wall, and boxes overflowing with files stood stacked in a corner. On the large table in the center of the room, next to Fenton's father's laptop computer, were the spine fossils—several chunks of bone, similar to the neck bones out at the excavation site, but larger, that fitted together into a row. Fenton pulled out a chair and sat down to look at them.

It took him a moment or two to find the small indentations, but sure enough, just as he expected, they were there—several tiny scratchlike grooves all along the edges of the thick chunks of spine bone. Fenton ran his hand along the grooves,

71

thinking. Obviously these were the same type of marks as the ones he had seen on all the other bones.

"Fenton!" called his father from outside. "It's time for us to head home. Why don't you let me give you a ride down the mountain in the truck?"

"Just a minute, Dad!" Fenton called back, hurriedly opening his sketchbook. He made a quick drawing of the spine bones, being careful to record the scratch marks exactly.

"Fenton?" said Mr. Rumplemayer again a few moments later. He pushed open the door to the trailer and peered inside. "Are you ready? Come on, son. Let's go."

"Okay, Dad," said Fenton, sketching in the last few marks and quickly flipping his sketchbook shut.

11

"Okay, everybody," said Fenton, looking around at the people gathered at the dining-room table. "I suppose you're probably wondering why I asked you all to come here."

"Yes, Fenton," said Professor Martin. "As a matter of fact, we are."

"What's this important announcement you say you have, son?" asked Mr. Rumplemayer.

"Really," said Charlie. "Why don't you let us in on the big secret?"

"Yeah, Fen," said Maggie. "What's up?"

Fenton cleared his throat. "I asked you all to come because I wanted to tell you that I, Fenton Rumplemayer"—he took a deep breath—"have finally *solved* the mystery of the dig site dinosaur's identity."

"Really?" said Willy, his eyes growing wider.

"That's great, Fen," said Maggie.

"Wonderful news," agreed Professor Martin.

"Well, son, what is it?" asked Fenton's father.

"Yes, tell us," said Charlie.

"Okay," said Fenton, taking a seat. "The answer is . . ." He thought a moment. "The dinosaur's identity is . . ." But suddenly his mind went blank, and he couldn't remember what it was he wanted to say.

"Fen?" said Maggie. "Are you all right?"

"I thought you were going to solve the mystery," said Willy. "What happened?"

Fenton shifted in his chair and heard it creak.

"Uh, I was, but now I can't remember," he said.

"Can't remember? What do you mean?" asked Professor Martin.

"Yeah," said Charlie, chuckling. "That's a mighty big thing to let slip your mind, Fenton."

Fenton moved uneasily in his chair and heard it creak beneath him again. He had been certain he knew the answer to the mystery, but now he couldn't seem to remember a thing. He looked around at the people gathered at the table and opened his mouth, waiting. But nothing came out. No one said anything; in fact, the only sound Fenton could hear was the chair beneath him creaking over and over.

Suddenly Fenton opened his eyes. He wasn't in the dining room at all, but in his own bedroom. Everything was dark, except for a beam of moonlight that came through one window and illuminated the end of his bed.

Fenton picked up the T-rex alarm clock from his night table and held it under the shaft of moonlight. Ten after three. He must have been dreaming. But it had all seemed so real; he really thought he had solved the mystery, and he could have sworn he had actually heard the chair creaking beneath him.

Just then he heard it again, a high-pitched squeak of some kind, almost like a whine or a cry, coming from outside. Almost immediately Fenton realized what it was—Owen! It wasn't a chair at all; it was Owen, crying.

Fenton hopped out of bed, hurried to the window, and peered out toward the trees behind the house. If Owen kept it up, he was sure to wake Fenton's father. Fenton knew he had to do something right away.

Quickly Fenton slipped his feet into his sneakers and pulled a sweatshirt over his pajamas. Slowly and quietly he opened his desk drawer and took out the flashlight inside. He tiptoed across his bedroom floor, being careful not to wake his father in the bedroom below him. Tucking the flashlight under one arm, Fenton climbed slowly down the ladder from his attic bedroom, tiptoed through the study, and went downstairs.

Fenton let himself out the side door, turned on his flashlight, and made his way across the backyard toward the trees in the distance. He could still hear Owen whimpering. Poor guy,

thought Fenton. He must be lonely and scared out there all by himself.

"Shhh. Quiet, boy," said Fenton, following the beam of the flashlight through the trees.

When Fenton finally found Owen, he could hardly believe his eyes. Somehow the poor dog had managed to completely tangle himself up in his rope. It was wrapped around the tree several times, and some of it was even twisted around Owen's legs. In fact, there was so little rope left free that Owen could hardly move at all.

The moment Owen saw him, though, he stopped crying and began to bark and wag his tail.

"Shhh," said Fenton again, bending down to pet him. "Quiet, boy."

Owen stopped barking, wagged his tail even harder, and tried to lick Fenton's face.

"Come on," said Fenton. "Let's get you untangled."

Fenton untied the rope from Owen's neck and unwrapped it from his legs.

"Okay, okay," he said, laughing, as the dog showered him with grateful kisses. "You're welcome."

Fenton looked around, trying to decide what to do. It seemed he had no choice but to bring Owen back to the house with him.

"All right, come on, boy," he sighed.

Owen leapt to his feet and began wagging his tail.

"Now, you'd better keep quiet," said Fenton, shaking a finger at the dog.

Owen looked up at him without making a sound, as if he understood.

They got back to the house and made their way through the living room toward the stairs. Owen was very quiet, but as soon as they were off the living-room carpet, his nails began to click loudly on the hardwood floor.

"Oh, no," Fenton whispered, stopping for a moment. He knew he couldn't take any chances that he might wake his father up. There was only one thing to do.

"Come on, boy," Fenton whispered. He put the flashlight on the bottom step, crouched down, and put his arms around Owen's body. "Up we go."

Fenton struggled to his feet with Owen in his arms. The dog was heavy, but the first set of stairs wasn't too difficult. Fenton kept whispering in Owen's ear, reminding him to keep quiet, and before he knew it they had reached the top. It was the second set of stairs, the ladderlike ones that led to Fenton's room, that was going to be really tough.

By this time Owen was getting really heavy, but Fenton knew he had to make it up to his room. He took a deep breath, managed to free one hand, and pulled himself up onto the first step. Owen groaned quietly as Fenton shifted him in his arm.

Little by little Fenton managed to make his way up the steep stairs. Finally, when he was a bit more than halfway up, and his eyes were just level with the floor of the attic, he gave Owen one enormous shove into his room and climbed up quickly behind him.

Owen seemed to love his new surroundings. He ran around Fenton's bedroom, sniffing things and wagging his tail happily. But Fenton knew that all that running was bound to wake his father below.

"Come on, boy. Come on, Owen," he said, patting the bed. "Come on up."

Owen leapt happily onto the bed, turned around once in place, and lay down at the far end.

"Good boy," said Fenton, kicking off his sneakers, pulling off his sweatshirt, and climbing under the covers.

He looked down at the dog curled up in the beam of moonlight.

"Good night, Owen," he whispered.

12

"Fenton! Fenton!" Mr. Rumplemayer shouted up the stairs. "Aren't you going to come down and have breakfast?"

"Um, I don't think so, Dad," Fenton called back. He looked at Owen, who was still sitting at the foot of his bed and had begun to whine. "Quiet," he whispered.

"Are you sure?" asked his father. "I don't know if that's such a good idea—going without breakfast."

"But I'm just not that hungry this morning, Dad," answered Fenton.

Fenton heard footsteps below.

"Shhh," he reminded Owen.

"Son?" his father called. "Are you feeling okay? Maybe I should come up and take a look at you."

"No! No!" Fenton cried. "I mean, I'm fine, Dad. That's okay. You just stay downstairs."

"Well, all right," said Mr. Rumplemayer. "If you're sure. But maybe you should let me give you a ride to school today. It looks like it could rain."

"No, no, that's okay," said Fenton. "I'd rather just ride my bike as usual." He sighed. Wasn't his father *ever* going to leave for work?

"All right then," said Mr. Rumplemayer. "I'll see you later on this evening, unless you decide to come by the dig site this afternoon."

"Okay, Dad," called Fenton, relieved. "Bye." He looked at Owen. "Phew, that was close."

But a few moments later, his father was back.

"Fenton?"

"Yes, Dad?" Fenton answered.

"I was just wondering if you knew what that flashlight was doing at the bottom of the stairs," his father.

"Oh, that?" said Fenton. "Well, you see, I—I got hungry last night, and I went downstairs to get a snack. I didn't want to turn on the lights and wake you, so I used the flashlight. I guess I must have left it down there."

"Well, well," said his father. "Snacking in the middle of the night—no wonder you're not hungry for breakfast, son."

"Yeah," said Fenton. "I guess that's it. Well, bye, Dad."

"Bye, Fenton," said Mr. Rumplemayer. "Don't be late for school."

I'm trying not to be, said Fenton to himself. And if you would just leave for work, I might not be.

Actually, Fenton felt kind of bad lying to his father like that. But he knew he had no choice if he wanted to help Owen. He just couldn't tell his father the truth about the dog.

Fenton heard his father's truck pull out of the driveway. He got off the bed to go downstairs. Owen jumped down too, wagging his tail.

"Okay, boy," said Fenton, heading for the opening in his floor that led to the steps. "Here we go."

Getting Owen down the attic stairs was at least as difficult as carrying him up had been, especially since the dog was licking Fenton's face the entire time. Once they were in the study, Fenton put Owen on the floor.

"Come on, boy," he said, leading Owen downstairs to the kitchen.

Fenton looked in the kitchen cabinets. "Sorry, Owen, but you're going to have to have cereal for breakfast," he said. "I'll try to get you some dog food soon, I promise."

He took out a box of cereal and poured it into two bowls, putting one on the floor for Owen and pouring milk into the other for himself.

Just then he heard Willy's voice from out in the backyard.

"Fenton! You ready to leave for school?" Willy called.

Fenton stuck his head out the kitchen window. "In a couple of minutes. Come on inside."

"Hey," said Willy, stepping into the kitchen and looking down at Owen, who was busy taking cereal out of his bowl and carrying it to the other side of the room to eat. "What's Owen doing here?"

82

"Well, he was crying last night, so I went out and got him," explained Fenton, taking a bite of his own cereal.

"Cool," said Willy. "So your father said it was okay?"

"Not exactly," said Fenton. "My father still doesn't know about him. I kept him in my room last night and this morning until my dad left."

"Wait a minute, Fenton," said Willy. "You can't just keep a dog hidden in your room forever."

"I know," said Fenton. "I guess I'll have to figure something out."

"Fenton, you've been saying that for days," Willy reminded him. "Listen, I hate to say it, but maybe it's time to face up to the fact that you might not be able to keep this dog after all."

Fenton felt his cereal stick in his throat. Deep down, he knew that Willy was probably right, but he hated to admit it.

"So, what's happening out at the dig site, Fen?" asked Maggie as she, Willy, and Fenton sat down in the school yard and opened their lunches later that day.

"Not much," said Fenton, taking a bite of his peanut butter and jelly sandwich. "My dad and the others still haven't been able to figure out anything."

"Too bad," said Willy, unwrapping his own sandwich.

"Yeah," said Fenton, thinking of his dream of the night before, the one where everyone had been gathered at the dining table to hear him solve the mystery. "My dad says if they can't identify the dinosaur, the museum probably won't even display the fossils."

"It sure is weird," said Maggie. "You know, the way the hip and the jawbone don't make sense together. It kind of makes you wonder . . ."

"Wonder?" repeated Fenton.

"Well, yeah," said Maggie. "Wonder if there's some other explanation. Something your dad and the others missed somehow."

"Well," said Fenton, thinking of the sketches he had made the day before, "now that you mention it . . ."

"What?" said Maggie, turning quickly to look at him. "Is there something you haven't told us, Fen?"

"Do you know what kind of dinosaur it was?" asked Willy excitedly.

"No, no, nothing like that," said Fenton. "It's just that I noticed these strange marks on the bones."

"Marks?" said Maggie. "What kind of marks?"

"I don't really know what they are," said Fenton. "But they almost look like some kind of scratches or something. They're really small; in fact, I don't think anyone else has even noticed them."

"Wow," said Willy. "What do you think they mean?"

"Beats me," said Fenton, shaking his head. "When I first noticed them on the pubis and the jawbone, I didn't really think anything of them. But when I realized there were some on the neck and spine bones too, I began to think they might be important somehow. I still haven't been able to figure out what they are or how they fit in, though."

"Hmmm," said Maggie, taking a bite of a carrot stick. "Sounds pretty mysterious. This is a tough one to figure out, Fen."

"Hey, Fenton," said Willy, "speaking of tough things to figure out, have you decided what you're going to do with Owen yet?"

"Really," said Maggie. "Where are you going to keep him?"

"Well," said Fenton, "for today I left him at my house, since my dad'll be at the dig site all day. But I guess I'm going to have to find somewhere else for him to stay." He sighed and took another bite of his sandwich.

"I'm really sorry it didn't work out for him at the ranch," said Maggie.

"Yeah, and I'm sorry he couldn't stay at the shack, either," said Willy.

"That's okay," said Fenton. "I guess it's about time I found Owen a *real* home anyway. He deserves to live in a real house, with people who love him."

"But how are you going to find someone to take him?" asked Willy.

"I know," said Maggie. "Why don't you make an announcement in assembly tomorrow."

"An announcement?" Fenton repeated.

85

"Sure," said Maggie. "People do it all the time. You could just say that you have this terrific dog and that you're looking for a home for him."

"Yeah," said Willy. "That's a good idea. I'm sure somebody will volunteer to take him in."

"Okay," said Fenton, popping the last of his sandwich into his mouth. "Great."

But he didn't feel great at all. In fact, whenever he thought about giving Owen away, he felt just terrible.

13

"Owen!" Fenton called loudly as he walked into the house after school that day. "Owen, where are you?" he called again, making his way down the hall to the living room. "I got you some dog food, boy!" He held up the plastic shopping bag from the Morgan Market. "Where are you?"

Just then Fenton heard a low grunting sound from somewhere nearby.

"Owen?" he called again. "Owen, is that you?"

A shiny black nose appeared from under the couch.

"Owen," Fenton said, laughing. "What are you doing under there, fella?"

He bent down and peered under the couch. There, lying on his stomach, was Owen, grunting with pleasure as he happily chewed on what was left of an old corncob. Nearby were several dried-out chicken bones, an empty tuna can, a candy wrapper, and an empty ice-cream container.

"Oh, no," said Fenton.

Owen must have dragged all of this stuff from the garbage in the kitchen and brought it out here to the living room to chew on, he realized.

"Owen," said Fenton, shaking his finger at the dog, "why did you do that?"

Owen stopped chewing the corncob and looked up at him guiltily. Again, it was as if he understood every word that Fenton said.

"Now I have to clean all this up because of you," said Fenton, sighing.

He reached under the couch and picked up the bones, the wrapper, and the can and put them in the ice-cream container. Owen looked up at him and, as if he knew what he had done wrong and was sorry, nudged the corncob toward Fenton with his nose.

Fenton picked up the cob, which was streaked with bite barks.

"Boy," he said, looking at Owen, "you're some chewer. Okay, come in the kitchen with me, Owen, and I'll give you something much better to eat."

Fenton walked back into the kitchen, with Owen trotting closely behind him. Sure enough, the trash can had been tipped over on its side, and trash was all over the floor. Fenton scooped the garbage back inside the can and set it upright again. Then, pulling the can of dog food out of the bag, he reached into a drawer for a can opener.

As Fenton spooned the dog food from the can into a bowl, Owen jumped up excitedly, putting his paws on the counter.

"That's right, boy," said Fenton, scraping the last of the food from the can. "This will taste much better to you than that nasty old garbage."

He reached over Owen and put the bowl down on the floor. As Owen hurried over to the bowl and gulped the food hungrily, Fenton shook his head.

"There you go, fella," he said. "Now you won't need to hunt around in the garbage like some kind of scavenger."

Suddenly Fenton thought of something.

"Like some kind of *scavenger!*" he repeated excitedly, his mind racing. "Oh my gosh, that's it!"

Fenton looked wildly around the room. He had to get out to the dig site right away. As fast as he could, he hurried out of the kitchen and down the hall. Bursting out onto the porch and stumbling down the steps, he ran toward his bike, which was leaning against the garage.

He was in such a hurry that he never even noticed that he had left the side door to the house wide open behind him.

14

"I've got it! I've got it!" Fenton repeated to himself excitedly, riding quickly toward the dig site.

The road up the mountain was steep and the sun was hot on his back, but the thought of what he had to say made him pedal harder and harder. This was definitely the fastest Fenton had ever ridden up the mountain; he could feel the muscles in his legs aching, but he kept going. He could hardly wait to see the looks on his father's and the other paleontologists' faces when he announced that he had solved the mystery at last. It would be just like in his dream, only it would be at the dig site instead of around the dining-room table—and, of course, this time Fenton wouldn't forget what he was going to say.

Suddenly he noticed a rock about the size of a baseball on the road in front of him. Fenton swerved, trying to avoid it, and his bicycle skidded out of control. He tried wildly to regain his balance, but he was too late, and the bicycle slid toward a shallow ditch on the side of the road.

"Ouch!" yelled Fenton as he landed hard in the ditch with his bicycle on top of him and his right leg twisted strangely beneath him. He pushed the bicycle to the side and looked down. Both of his hands were badly scraped, and there was a gaping hole in the knee of his jeans.

Brushing the gravel off his hands, he pulled his right leg out from under him. That's when he noticed it—a terrible pain in his ankle.

"Ouch!" said Fenton again, reaching down to rub his ankle. But touching it only made it hurt more.

I have to get up and get back on my bike, Fenton thought. But as the pain in his ankle grew, he wondered if he'd even be able to stand. He pushed himself up onto the knee of his good leg and tentatively put some weight on the injured ankle. But as soon as he did, the pain went shooting up his leg.

Fenton collapsed again on the ground. There was no way he could get anywhere on this ankle, he realized. It was probably sprained, or maybe even broken.

Fenton looked around and began to worry a little. Sleeping Bear Mountain Road wasn't exactly a busy thoroughfare; what if no one came by to help him?

Maybe he could manage to walk if he leaned on his bike. But as he turned toward it, Fenton saw that the front wheel was twisted. There was no way it would even be able to turn. Besides, the pain in his ankle was getting worse, and Fenton doubted he'd even be able to get up at all.

He could try to crawl. But which way should he go? He was already more than halfway to the dig site, but the rest of the way was all uphill. He could try to get home instead, but that was a pretty long way; it would probably be dark by the time he made it.

Fenton took a deep breath and tried to stay calm. If worse came to worst and no one passed by, at least he could count on the fact that his father and the others would be driving down the mountain later on, right? But sometimes they didn't stop digging until it started getting dark, Fenton remembered. How could he be sure that his father would see him from his truck if the sun was going down?

Just then Fenton heard a familiar tapping sound. The tapping grew louder, and he turned his head. There, running up the road, headed directly toward him, was Owen!

"Owen!" Fenton cried happily as Owen licked his face. "Good boy! Good dog!"

What an incredible feeling it was to see Owen's familiar furry face. Fenton put his arms around the dog and hugged him in relief. But then he realized—what could Owen really do to help him? It wasn't like the dog could carry him home, or go get help. Or *could* he?

Fenton looked at Owen. He had always had the feeling that the dog understood what he was saying; here was a chance to put it to the test. After all, Owen had brought the stick to Willy that day when Fenton had told him to, hadn't he?

93

"Owen," said Fenton. "You've got to listen to me, boy. I'm hurt, and I need you to go get help." He pointed to his ankle.

Owen leaned down to sniff Fenton's ankle. He looked back up at Fenton and barked.

This is ridiculous, thought Fenton. What makes me think that Owen is really going to be able to understand me? I'm acting like I think we're Powerboy and Lightning, or something. But I have no choice, he realized. Right now Owen is my only hope.

"Listen here, boy," Fenton tried again. "Go to Willy, okay? *Willy*, remember?"

At the mention of Willy's name, Owen pricked up his ears.

"That's it," said Fenton. "*Willy!* Go get Willy, Owen, okay?"

Owen glanced back down the road in the direction of Fenton's and Willy's houses.

"Yes!" cried Fenton. "That's right, boy! Go get Willy! Go on! Get Willy!"

The next thing Fenton knew, Owen was headed off down the road. The dog turned once to look back, and Fenton waved him on.

Fenton watched the dog disappear down the road. Could it be that he had actually understood what Fenton had said?

The next hour felt like the longest of Fenton's whole life. Not one car drove by, and the throbbing in his ankle was getting worse. I guess it was pretty stupid of me to be riding so fast, he thought. But he had been in such a hurry to get to the

dig site and tell his father and the others his good news. Now he couldn't help wondering how long it would be before he saw his father—or anyone else—again.

Then he heard the shift of bicycle gears behind him. He turned his head and could hardly believe what he saw. There, headed up the road toward him, was Willy on his bike!

"Fenton! Oh my gosh, what happened?" said Willy, dropping his bike and hurrying over to Fenton's side. "Are you all right?"

"I fell off my bike," said Fenton. "And I think I hurt my ankle pretty bad."

"Oh, wow," said Willy, looking concerned. "Do you want me to help you get up?"

"I don't think I can stand on it," said Fenton. "I guess you'd better ride up the mountain and get my dad."

"Okay, sure, no problem," said Willy, picking up his bike. "But are you going to be okay here?"

"Yeah," sighed Fenton. "Just hurry, all right?"

"All right," said Willy, climbing on his bike. "Gee, it sure is lucky I rode up here."

"Hey, why *did* you come up here, Willy?" asked Fenton.

"Actually, it was Owen," said Willy.

"Owen?" repeated Fenton, managing a smile.

"Yeah," said Willy. "It was the strangest thing. He showed up at my house, and he was barking like crazy. I figured he must have got out of your house somehow, so I took him back to your place and put him inside. When you weren't there, I thought you might have gone out to the dig site, so I decided to ride out and find you. I thought maybe there might be some news about the dinosaur."

"There is, Willy," said Fenton. "I think I solved the mystery."

"Hey, that's great, Fenton, but you can tell me all about it later," said Willy, pushing off on his bike. "Right now I'd better get up the mountain and get you some help."

15

"All right now, be careful," said Fenton's father as they made their way across the hospital parking lot. He helped Fenton into the passenger side of the pickup truck. "Watch out for that cast, son."

Fenton slid into the truck and laid his crutches down on the seat next to him. His father made his way around the truck and opened the other door.

"Are you okay?" asked his father, taking his place behind the wheel.

"Yeah, Dad, I'm fine," said Fenton.

"Well, you certainly won't be riding out to the dig site for a few weeks," said Mr. Rumplemayer, closing the truck door. "Or doing much else, for that matter. Not till that broken ankle heals."

"Yeah, I know," said Fenton. He sighed. No visits to the dig site! What was he going to do?

"And I think we ought to have a little talk about bicycle safety, too, son," said Mr. Rumplemayer, starting the engine and pulling out onto the road.

"Oh, Dad," said Fenton, "I'm a safe bike rider. Really. I've never even had an accident before. It's just that this time I was in a big hurry, so I didn't see the rock in the road until it was too late. You see, I had something really important that I wanted to tell you right away."

"Fenton," said his father sternly, "nothing is so important that it's worth risking hurting yourself over. You ought to know that. This could have been even more serious than it was. You're just lucky that Willy came along when he did. Now, what was this thing you say you wanted to tell me?"

"Well," said Fenton, eyeing his father, "I think I may have figured out the explanation for those confusing fossils out at the dig site."

"Oh?" said his father, raising his eyebrows.

"Yeah," said Fenton. "Listen to this. You say that the dinosaur was fossilized in the ash of a volcano, right?"

"That's correct," said Fenton's father.

"Well, the way I see it, just because we found it in volcanic ash doesn't mean that was where it died," said Fenton.

"What do you mean, son?" asked Mr. Rumplemayer. "It seems like the logical explanation, doesn't it? It's not as if the animal could move around *after* it died."

"Maybe it could, though, Dad," said Fenton. "Or rather, maybe something else could have moved it. Or moved pieces of it."

"Something else?" Fenton's father repeated.

"Right," said Fenton. "Like a scavenger—an animal that eats parts of other animals that are already dead."

"Interesting idea, son," said Mr. Rumplemayer.

"Maybe the scavenger brought the pieces to another area to eat them," said Fenton. "Lots of times animals who scavenge will bring all the stuff they find back to some special place where they can chew on it." He paused. "For instance, dogs do that all the time."

"True," agreed Mr. Rumplemayer.

"So," said Fenton, "the way I figure it, some kind of scavenger could have taken pieces from more than one dinosaur— like the hip from a small saurischian and the jaw from an ornithischian about the same size—and brought them back to the same place to eat them. Then a volcano erupted nearby, covering the pieces with ash."

"Hmmm," said his father. "I think you may just have something there, Fenton."

"Now you know why I was in such a hurry to get to the dig site," said Fenton, grinning.

"Yes," said his father, pulling the truck onto the turnoff for their house, "I do see. But I do have one more question, Fenton."

"Sure, Dad, what is it?" said Fenton.

"How did Willy happen to know that you were in trouble out there on the road?" asked his father. "I mean, he wasn't with you when you first left for the dig site, so what made him ride out there and find you like that?"

Fenton looked at his father and took a deep breath.

"Well, Dad," he said, "now that we're home, I guess there's somebody you should meet. Someone who I think will probably be able to help me answer that question for you."

16

"Okay," said Maggie as she, Willy, Fenton, and the paleontologists sat around the Rumplemayers' dining-room table a week later, eating dinner. "So let me get this straight. There were actually *two* dinosaurs?"

"That's right," said Fenton's father, passing the platter of fried chicken to her. "From the rest of the bones that turned up, we were able to tell that the hip bone and the spine bones we found were both from a troodon, a small saurischian meat-eater."

"Troodon," said Maggie, taking a chicken leg from the platter. "They're the ones with the big brains, right?"

"Right," said Fenton, stretching out his leg and resting his cast on the empty chair next to him. He buttered himself a biscuit. "Some people think they were the smartest of the dinosaurs."

"So what dinosaur were the other bones from, then?" asked Maggie.

"Both the jawbone and the neck bones turned out to be from a stegoceras," said Professor Martin, shaking out her napkin. "It's an ornithischian dinosaur that's a member of the pachycephalosaur family."

"Those are the head-butters, right?" asked Maggie.

"Yeah," said Fenton. "They had these incredibly thick skulls and these really small brains. Some scientists think that pachycephalosaurs used to smash their heads together. They probably weren't too bright."

"They don't sound it," said Willy, laughing.

"One of the things that had us so confused was that the two dinosaurs were basically the same size," said Mr. Rumplemayer. "So, because we knew that we were dealing with fossils that had been trapped in volcanic ash, we made the mistake of assuming that the bones were all from the same animal."

"When, actually, the bones of the two dinosaurs were brought together by the scavenger, who had torn off bits of the animals and dragged them off to chew on them," said Professor Martin.

"Which is how all those little scratch marks got on the fossils," said Fenton. "They were bite marks, from the scavenger's chewing."

"I still can't believe we missed those," said Charlie, shaking his head. "Nice work, Fenton."

"Yes, son," said Mr. Rumplemayer. "Good thinking on your part."

"I'm curious," said Professor Martin, helping herself to a biscuit. "How did you figure it out, Fenton? What was it that made you come up with the idea of a scavenger?"

"Actually," said Fenton, "the credit for that should really go to my partner."

"Your partner?" said Professor Martin.

"Sure," said Fenton, grinning. "Would you like to meet him?"

"Why, certainly," said Professor Martin.

"Okay," said Fenton. He leaned back from the table. "Owen!" he called. "Owen, come here, boy!"

Owen trotted into the room, wagging his tail, and dropped the rawhide bone he was carrying.

"Professor Martin, I'd like you to meet my partner, Owen," said Fenton.

"Oh," said Professor Martin. "I didn't realize you had a dog."

"Yes, it looks as if we do," said Mr. Rumplemayer. "Frankly, I'm nearly as surprised by it as you are."

"Well, isn't that nice," said Professor Martin. "It's wonderful to have a pet, don't you think? There's nothing like caring for an animal to teach responsibility."

Fenton looked at his father.

"Yes, I suppose you're right," said Mr. Rumplemayer, smiling. "That's a very interesting way of looking at it, Professor Martin." He reached out to stroke Owen's head.

Fenton took a bite of his chicken and gazed happily around the room. Things couldn't be better, he thought. His ankle would be healed in a little while, Owen was staying after all, and the dinosaur mystery had been solved at last.

In fact, thought Fenton, looking around the dining-room table at the people gathered there, it was almost like a dream come true.

After about fifteen minutes of digging, Max sat back on his heels.

"I don't think there's anything here, Fenton," he said.

Charlie chuckled. "Well, you probably have to give it a little more of a chance than that, Max."

"Yeah," said Fenton. "Like I said, sometimes it takes a while to uncover fossils."

Max sighed and went back to work. But ten minutes later he stopped again.

"I don't think I'm going to do any more. My hands are starting to hurt."

"They'll get use to it soon," said Fenton, still digging away.

"No, really," said Max, putting down his pick. "I think I'm starting to get blisters."

"Are you sure, Max?" he asked. "I mean, you could miss out on being part of a really important discovery."

"Yeah, I think I'll just sit and watch for a while," said Max.

Fenton had to admit he was pretty disappointed. It was starting to seem as if he and Max had hardly anything in common at all anymore. Had Max changed, or was it Fenton who was different now? If only Max would at least try to get along in Morgan, thought Fenton. But there was no doubt about it; Max may have been his best friend in New York, but in Wyoming he was starting to seem completely out of place.

Look for **DINOSAUR DETECTIVE #4** and the rest of the series in your local bookstore, or call toll-free number 1-800-877-5351.

Join Fenton Rumplemayer in more of his awesome adventures in the Dinosaur Detective series.

#1 *On the Right Track*

Fenton feels out of place when he first moves to Wyoming. But when a mysterious set of dinosaur tracks turns up, he's right at home. Hooked up by computer to his old pal Max in New York, and ably assisted by a new friend, Fenton tackles a case that has the local scientific team baffled.

#2 *Fair Play*

Fenton is the new kid in his class in Wyoming, and the bully has chosen him to pick on. But Fenton and his new friend Maggie have a great project for this year's Dinosaur Fair, and they're hot on the trail of a fossil that's missing from his father's dinosaur dig. Can Fenton and his friends find the missing piece, foil the bully, and still have their project ready in time for the fair?

#3 *Bite Makes Right*

Can a dinosaur be part bird-hipped and part lizard-hipped? That's sure what Professor Rumplemayer's new fossil find looks like. Fenton is stumped. And on top of that he's been adopted by a stray mutt that's making trouble for all of his friends. Can Fenton find a good home for the dog and solve the mystery?

#4 *Out of Place*

Max, Fenton's computer-whiz pal, comes from New York for Halloween. But the visit isn't as much fun as the boys expected. Max doesn't get along with Fenton's new friends, and he thinks the story of the town's founding is a big joke. He doesn't even like working at the dig site, where the paleontologists have found a dinosaur that seems misplaced in time.

Try some other dinosaur books from Scientific American *Books for Young Readers*—

Jack Horner: Living With Dinosaurs
by Don Lessem, from the new Science Superstars series.

Jack Horner found his first fossil when he was eight years old. From that day on, he knew exactly what he wanted to do when he grew up—study dinosaurs. But his dream looked like it was over after he flunked out of college—seven times!

Author Don Lessem, founder of the Dinosaur Society and a friend of Jack Horner's, tells the stranger-than-fiction story of a man who followed his own path to become one of the world's leading dinosaur experts, the real-life hero behind the scientist in the book and movie *Jurassic Park*.

Colossal Fossil
The Dinosaur Riddle Book by the Riddle King himself, Mike Thaler

- What dinosaur was a great boxer?
- What dinosaur played video games?
- What do you call a prehistoric Girl Scout?

Find the answers to these riddles and many more inside this wacky book about the most fascinating creatures to walk (shake?) the Earth.

**If you like the Dinosaur Detective series . . .
Join Mathnet Casebook detectives George Frankly and Pat
Tuesday as they use their powers of reasoning to crack
confounding cases—and jokes, too.**

#1 The Case of the Unnatural

Roy "Lefty" Cobbs is making a spectacular comeback for the River Vale Rowdies. His batting and pitching averages have never been better. In fact, they're too good to be true—which is why Lefty's pal Babs Bengal suspects foul play. DUM DEE DUM DUM.

#2 Despair in Monterey Bay

Lady Esther Astor Astute is in despair—and no wonder. Her priceless Despair Diamond has disappeared. The Mathnetters go undercover—and underwater—to catch the thief. But their case won't hold water until they turn to the tides. Something's fishy in Monterey Bay. DUM DEE DUM DUM.

#3 The Case of the Willing Parrot

The late great movie star Fatty Tissue left his mansion to his parrot. Now the wisecracking bird is doing some strange squawking. Is it one of Tissue's infamous math games or a clue to a much bigger mystery? Soon the Mathnetters are up to their Fibonacci numbers in haunted corridors, birdnapping, and cryptic messages, as a clever swindler tries to feather his own nest. DUM DEE DUM DUM.

#4 The Case of the Map With a Gap

Ten-year-old cowboy Bronco Guillermo Gomez is searching for the long lost loot of the notorious Saddlesore Capone. He knows it lies somewhere in the ghost town of Mulch Gulch. But he only has half of the treasure map, and someone sinister is on his trail. Can the Mathnetters help him fill in the gap? DUM DEE DUM DUM.

#5 *The Case of the Mystery Weekend*

George and Pat are going to play "Sherlock Condo" and "Dr. Whatzit" at a Mystery Weekend Party. But one wrong turn leads them to Wit's End, a sinister mansion presided over by the butler, Peeved. Strange things begin to happen as the guests disappear one by one. Who extracted Kitty Feline, world-renowned dentist? Who snipped short the song of jazzman Miles Reed? And how did soap star Sally Storm slip away? Can George and Pat out-math the mastermind behind it all? DUM DEE DUM DUM.

#6 *The Case of the Smart Dummy*

It's a case of mistaken cases! Ventriloquist Edgar Bergman is dumbfounded when he loses his luggage with Lolly, his dummy, inside. Instead, he's left holding the bag, and it's full of stolen money. The only one who's talking is Edgar's other dummy, Charlie McShtick, and he says Edgar is innocent. Is Edgar in the act or can Pat and George find out who's pulling the strings? DUM DEE DUM DUM.